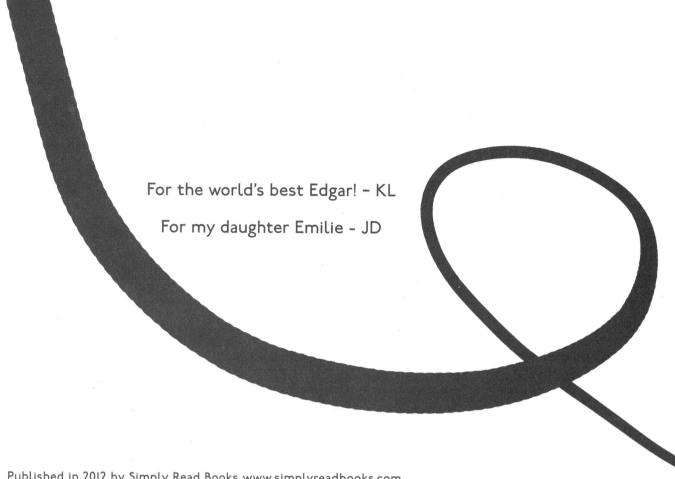

For the world's best Edgar! – KL

For my daughter Emilie – JD

Published in 2012 by Simply Read Books www.simplyreadbooks.com
Text © 2012 Kai Lüftner · Illustrations © 2012 Judith Drews

Library and Archives Canada Cataloguing in Publication
Lüftner, Kai
        Lily loves/ written by Kai Lüftner ; illustrated by Judith Drews.
ISBN 978-1-897476-94-9
 I. Drews, Judith II. Title.
PZ7.L849Wor 2012   j833'.92   C2011-906668-8

We gratefully acknowledge for their financial support of our publishing program the Canada Council for the Arts, the BC Arts Council, and the Government of Canada through the Canada Book Fund (CBF).

Manufactured in China

Design by Judith Drews, Cover design by Sara Gillingham

10 9 8 7 6 5 4 3 2 1

lily
loves

Kai Lüftner

Judith Drews

Lily is no longer little,
but she is not yet big either.

mother

father

Lily has her mother's eyes and her father's mouth.
Nevertheless, she is totally and truly herself.

When someone calls her
"my little Lily flower"
she gets very angry.
Even so, she always wears
a flower in her hair.

Lily loves stories that could never have happened
but are true all the same.

Lily doesn't like math, but she loves to paint numbers.

Lily is so strong she can squeeze water out of a stone
and tie knots in thick branches.
But she also is so gentle she can dance
on an egg without breaking it.

Lily loves her silky princess hair
that is also as wild as a lion's mane.
And she can be very funny... seriously funny.

Lily's favorite animals are guinea pigs.
And cats. And small dogs with soft fur and red collars.
And turtles. And, of course, horses.

Lily can frown so furiously that glass shatters.

But she can also smile so sweetly that snow melts.

Lily gets her freckles in the summer,
but she loves them so much she keeps them in winter, too.
She even names them.

marlene→

Lily doesn't think lying is good,
but she does tell a little fib once in a while just the same.

Lily has a big heart, although she is still quite small.
(Well, at least not so very big.)

Lily can scream so loudly
that the birds lose their feathers,

but she can also whisper so softly
that she can't hear herself.

Lily's name has only three different letters,
although it is actually made up of four.

Lily is the world's best Lily, says her mother.
And she thinks her mother is right.

One thing is for certain,
what the world's best Lily does next
is absolutely not certain.

You don't have to be named Lily
in order to be the world's best.

But you must know who you are and what you love...
and what you are not and what you don't love.

You are simply the world's best when you are who you are.
Does that sound complicated? It isn't at all.
Just look in a mirror and love yourself.
That's what Lily does everyday—no ands, ifs or buts about it.